GERMINATION

ALSO BY JAMIE THORNTON

ZOMBIES ARE HUMAN (Science Fiction)

Germination: Book 0

Contamination: Book 1

Infestation: Book 2

Eradication: Book 3

AFTER THE WORLD ENDS (Science Fiction)

Run: Book 1

Hide: Book 2

Find: Book 3

Save: Book 4 (coming soon)

Fight (coming soon)

Live (coming soon)

DOORMAKER (Science Fantasy)

Rock Heaven: Book 1

Tower of Shadows: Book 2

Library of Souls: Book 3

The One Door: Book 4

Devil's Harvest: A Prequel

Torchlighters: A Short Novel

IGNEOUS
BOOKS

PO Box 159
Roseville, CA 95678

Cover Art by Mayflower Studio
Copy edited by Melanie Lytle

Zombies Are Human Book Zero

GERMINATION

A Short Novel

Jamie Thornton

IGNEOUS
BOOKS

To all the readers who also ran **to** *their family*

SHOULD I RUN AWAY?

Posted August 10th at 5:36PM on Do More Than Survive: How to THRIVE as a Runaway

If you are asking that question and wonder what the answer is —the answer is no. It's not bad enough. Stick it out, whatever you're going through. It's more dangerous on the street.

If it doesn't matter what I say, you're going to run away— then read on.

Pros:

- *Lots of freedom and travel*
- *You will become very skilled at living outside*
- *You will meet lots of interesting people*

Cons:

- *If it's cold, you're going to be cold, if it's wet, even worse. If it's hot—you get the idea.*
- *If you are traveling between cities, sometimes you will go without food for several days.*
- *Lots of the interesting people you meet will want to steal from you, hurt you, or sell you something that will hurt you.*
- *If you look under sixteen it's going to be really hard for you to make money without getting into serious trouble.*
- *If there's anybody at home who still cares, like a little sister or a grandpa, you will seriously hurt them.*

If you're actually trying to thrive as a runaway, I don't recommend:

Stealing—if you get caught you go to jail which is worse than whatever home you left, but sometimes you need something, just don't expect to get away with it forever.

Drug dealing—you're likely to get hooked and become a tweeker, or get caught and go to jail. I'm not saying street kids don't deal drugs. It's fast money, but it's risky. If it's really about money for you, then why did you run away in the first place?

Prostitution—this is disgusting. People do it, but not me. Not ever. But sometimes you have to trade favors because you want a hot shower or a bed to sleep in and that's okay. Just don't make it a habit.

Believing in monsters—people will tell you so many rumors about monsters while you're on the street. Sometimes it even makes the news, like right now. It's true, there are monsters on the street. There have always been monsters on the street, but not like what the news is talking about. Don't let the stories scare you too bad—only just enough to find some others who will watch your back.

I'm not saying I haven't done any of the above. I'm saying I wish I hadn't. So it's better if you try to avoid it from the beginning. I hope you don't have to learn the hard way like I did. But if you do, I won't judge.

If you can endure it for a little longer, the older you are before you run away the better your chances at making money without resorting to sex, stealing, or other stuff that might hurt you or make you sick. I ran away when I was thirteen. I did a lot of stuff I wish I could take back. I'm almost seventeen now and thinking maybe I don't want to live on the street for the rest of my life.

Also, if you think you're going to find happiness by running away, you're dead wrong. Happiness comes from within.

If you run away, all your demons go with you.

Just saying this because I know. But I'm not telling you not to run. I did it after all, which is why I'm writing about it—to maybe help those like me who are going to run no matter what.

If you're still fed up and it's time to go, then this blog is for you.

1

THE GUY, MIDDLE-AGED, WEARING business casual, probably walking home from work, held out a dollar like it stank.

The cell phone lay in plain sight between me and Gabbi on the hot sidewalk. Seconds before Mr. Casual had shown up, I'd hit submit on two posts scheduled to go live an hour apart —my readers expected constant updates. And anyways, if someone were thinking right then about running away, they couldn't exactly wait a week to read my next one, could they?

"Thank you, sir. Thank you so much." Gabbi actually said it without any sarcasm in her voice, which was more than I'd have bet she could manage with his holier-than-thou attitude.

Their hands hovered in mid-air—hers, dirt-streaked, with half-moon lines under the nails. She grabbed for the green bill.

His pale, clean hand didn't let go.

I looked up. His gaze was locked on a spot near Gabbi's knee.

On the phone.

"What are you two playing at here?"

Gabbi folded her hands in her lap, her back straight, her round face and brown eyes expressionless.

The phone had been free, someone's discard. We loaded it when there was extra cash. I liked posting more than the public library allowed, plus it kept us in touch with the rest of the group. But he wouldn't understand. None of them ever did. "We're good people. We just need some help," I said.

"You stole that."

"A first generation iPhone?" I said, not being able to stop myself. "Please. I would have stolen something newer than that."

You could almost see him get madder even though he didn't say a word. He stalked off a few steps, stopped. Looked down the street, started to come back.

Damn.

Between the window washing job I'd finished yesterday and today's spanging money, we almost had enough for Jimmy's birthday cake, some gas for the van, and this month's gym membership. Clearly we weren't getting any money out of Mr. Casual. The faster he left the better. This was a good spot, but only during rush hour.

Plus, we both feared Norman would appear at any moment to take back his corner. Street rumors said someone or something had murdered him in a weirdly gruesome way.

You had to figure people would exaggerate. But still.

A red four-door drove through the intersection and then another handful of cars all in a row. The light turned yellow and the cars began to slow, but Mr. Casual blocked them from our view. He stepped closer into our space. His cologne was so thick I wondered if he secretly liked to suffocate people.

"What do you want?" Gabbi said, all thankfulness gone now. I'd taught her that early on—be super nice when people help you out, otherwise get aggro.

"You two, out on the street like this, begging. It's disgusting. You think it's funny, acting like you're hard up?"

"We are hard up," I said, fiddling with the braided end of my hair. We got more money when I let my black hair down to offset my dark eyes and brows, but it was too hot for that.

"You should be in school. I work hard for my money. What do you do? Beg like this?"

"Don't give us your money," I said, tugging on my braid until it hurt. "Go home to your wife and 2.3 kids and your TV and your mortgage. We don't need your help. You don't even know—"

"Is this what you always wanted—to be homeless?"

"We're not homeless," I said. "A homeless kid stays at a shelter and never leaves the neighborhood where they got left. We're travelers. We left. We're out here, seeing the world and what it's really like and all the cool people in it, and sometimes all the dicks in it like you."

He stopped listening to me and pointed at Gabbi as if somehow sensing he was getting to her. "Where are your parents? They should know you're pretending, taking peoples' money just for kicks. Your parents must be disappointed in you. They must have hoped you would become so much more than this." He jabbed his finger into Gabbi's face.

She seemed to melt into the sidewalk. Each word made her head sink lower until her forehead was inches from the sidewalk, as if in an ashamed bow.

Crashing waves of air filled my ears. I lost feeling in my toes and my hands began to shake.

How dare he.

How dare he put that look on her face.

I jumped up and pushed him hard in the chest. My hands left dark imprints from sweat and dirt on his clean, pale blue shirt.

The flush of his forehead deepened into a purplish-red. His blonde hair was stringy, in one of those styles where you could see the pink flesh of scalp underneath.

"We were nice to you. We didn't point any fingers. We didn't harass you. You think you know her?" I pushed him again and he stumbled back a few inches. "You think you can talk to her like that because you were going to give us one stinking dollar?"

"Young lady, you should be ashamed—"

"You better stop right now." I clenched my hands at my sides and dared him to say something else, anything.

He opened his mouth, closed it. He backed up a step, then a second one. "I'm calling the police." He left quickly, rounding the corner.

The light turned. The cars, filled with people pretending not to look, disappeared in a thick cloud of exhaust.

I tried to calm the roar in my ears.

Gabbi hadn't moved.

"Gabbi." I brushed my hair off my face and realized my hands now smelled like his cologne. I spit on them, rubbed in the spit, and then wiped the smell as best I could onto the newspaper. "He's a jerk. He's a 9-to-5 wage slave who knows nothing about you or me or anything. Forget him. Stand up for yourself next time. You'll feel better about someone being a jerk if you're a jerk back."

"I'm fine," she said after a long second.

"Come on." I touched her shoulder. "We need to move." No doubt Mr. Casual was already calling the cops. I decided I would find a way to make her laugh. God knows we both needed it.

I gathered up the newspapers we used to keep our pants off the gum-pocked sidewalk. Gabbi slipped the phone into a zippered pants pocket. Both of us wore our spanging shirts—ratty, threadbare things we kept dirty. People gave more money to kids who really looked the part. The dirt I had sifted into Gabbi's hair had caked into mud a while ago. My long dark hair washed out pretty easily. Gabbi's light brown frizz was a different story. At least the newspapers grimed up our hands in an easy-to-wash-off way. We'd go by 24 Hour Fitness later and clean up.

A couple of blocks away, I set down our jar and sign and we folded ourselves against the wall of a corner liquor store. Gabbi moved into the shade to keep herself from burning. I didn't like the heat, but my skin never burned, it only turned a darker cinnamon.

I sighed. Spanging was the crappiest job ever.

We made sure to hide the phone when a green Ford sedan slowed. The driver's side window hummed down, revealing a woman behind the wheel with a too-sunny smile even for summer.

"Can you spare any change?" I said, returning her smile. You had to smile, you had to be nice no matter how horrible you felt, and Gabbi wasn't that good at acting.

She held out a fiver. A gold bracelet caught the light, flashing us.

Gabbi jumped up, her shoulder-length hair frizzing like nobody's business.

"Thank you," I called out when Gabbi said nothing. "God bless you."

Their fingers brushed. She pulled back her manicured hand like she feared an animal was about to bite her.

The window rolled up and she drove off.

Gabbi returned to a cross-legged position. I leaned over and brushed a leaf from her shoulder then tugged her hair. "There are worse ways to earn money."

I didn't need to say it. I shouldn't have said it. We didn't need reminding about other ways we'd scrounged up cash in the past. But that was over. Things were going to be different now. "You know Jimmy's hankering for that special dark chocolate cake," I said, trying to change the subject.

"It feels dumb getting money for cake," Gabbi said. "Especially when we can get a whole box of day-old donuts for free."

"But he's desperate for it. You can't really hold it against him."

"Watch me." She harrumphed in that way of hers that tried to cover up how young she still was deep down, how she wanted to belong to somebody, just like the rest of us. But she would die before letting anyone know it. Her parents did that to her. They didn't throw her away like they did Leaf, but they drove her off all the same.

"He's still an oogle." I smiled and showed my teeth. "Like you were—not so long ago."

"Over a year!"

I realized I hadn't made her laugh yet. I decided to take this as a personal insult. "Being a runaway isn't so bad." I talked in my deepest, most reflective, most professorial tone to match that woman who had stalked us for two weeks. She had wanted to do a college paper on how life was really like for street kids. She kept asking about survival sex, and how often we did this drug or that drug, or how often we'd beaten somebody up, and how many murders we must have witnessed, and how much did we drink. She didn't want to know anything we really cared about, like how cramped the van got sometimes, and how we wanted more public library hours, and what were our favorite Tumblr blogs, and how at the last park concert Leaf got invited to drum on stage during the band's encore.

"Being a street kid means you get the freedom to party whenever you want and you don't have any college debt or responsibilities." I pushed imaginary glasses up my nose. Like taking care of our food, shelter, clothing, safety, hygiene, not getting pregnant, it was no big deal, true freedom, living it up.

Gabbi smiled—but I wanted her to laugh.

"It's not so bad, not if you're smart and careful and stay out of the drug houses, shelters, pimp control, gang territory, rich people territory, poor people territory, middle people territory. You know, all the territory." I leaned over and pantomimed opening a notepad while holding a pencil. "Now please tell me exactly how many blow jobs you gave in exchange for food this week."

Gabbi's laughter rang out like a bell. That helpless kind of laugh that started from the belly and shook the chest and made you hiccup at the end.

I toed the sidewalk and hid my smile. She'd be mad at me later for making her bust up like that, but it was worth it. She was fifteen, I was seventeen. But both of us liked to laugh as if we were little kids. I think it was partly because neither of us had laughed much when we were actually little.

Minutes passed. Only one car drove by. An old man popped into the liquor store before I could ask for change. This corner was slow.

The digital doorbell beeped again. The old man came out, his plastic bag boxy from a six-pack. He dropped some coins in the jar before I could say a word.

I tipped my head and smiled. "Thank you, sir."

He nodded. "I've been in your shoes once or twice. Good luck to you."

"Why can't they all be like that?" Gabbi said after he left. She sighed. "What do you think Spencer will find tonight?"

I leaned back against the wall, happy that at least someone didn't see us as worse than dirt. "Ano said he was going to swing by the bakery on O Street and try to score some day-olds. That's all I'm thinking about. And maybe buy some new toothbrushes."

"I'm pretty sure that's not all you're thinking about when it comes to Ano."

"Very funny," I said, but we both knew she was right, and mostly I didn't care since he was hot and really nice and we both had a thing for each other.

"Jimmy wants another disposable camera." Gabbi shook the jar, the coins clanging together amongst the dollars.

Jimmy was the newest to the group. I still hadn't decided if he was a lifer yet, or if he would end up going back to his family after playing street kid with us. But I suspected he was going to stay. Sometimes you can just tell.

"Heads-up," Gabbi said.

A man dirtier than us limped across the street. It looked like he'd come from the two-story office building that had been shut down for days—if the pile of newspapers at the door was any indication. His clothes were ragged, his shirt torn at the collar. His hair was cropped short but still somehow managed to look like a terrible case of bedhead.

No one else was in sight. The old guy was long gone. I jumped up and wondered if we should go into the liquor store and hide until the owner called the cops on us for loitering.

For all my jokes and lightheartedness, things could turn mean real fast. Thoughts of Norman came to mind. If he was back, he'd have already heard we'd been spanging on his corner. We'd be in for a beating for invading his territory. I didn't totally believe in angels anymore, not like I used to when I was a kid, but I still believed that demons were pretty much real—and Norman was a homeless one in human form.

"Is that—"

“Can’t tell.” Gabbi sat on the ground as if she didn’t have a care in the world. But her leg was too relaxed, her fingers too splayed out.

A lone car passed by, blasting hot air. The man tracked it, distracted by the movement or the engine noise. The car and its person and its chance for help disappeared. Silence returned. His right pant leg was ripped from the ankle to his thigh, revealing a bloody gash.

Sweat itched down my cheek. I wiped the bead away.

He turned in our direction now as if he had noticed my movement. As if he had smelled us. His hands spasmed open and closed around something small and bloody, like he had dipped wrist-deep into a bucket of blood and pulled out a heart or something.

My mother had always accused me of a vivid imagination —it was why she called me a liar when I said my stepdad had kicked me in the ribs for not getting him a beer one night. I hoped in this case that it actually was my imagination going wild.

“What’s that in his hand?” Gabbi said.

“Nothing good for us,” I said. It might not be a bloody heart, but that didn’t make him Mr. Nice Guy either.

Finally the sound of another engine appeared just as I decided we should risk the liquor store. I waved it down before realizing it was a black and white.

“You’ve got to be kidding me,” Gabbi said.

“Better than the creep.”

“Not really.”

Officer Hanley leaned over, showing off short, silver hair that still covered most of his head. Cops weren’t my favorite people. They kicked us out from underpasses, and harassed us off street corners, and confiscated our van if we didn't move it often enough. But Officer Hanley could sometimes be all right.

Cool air blasted through the open window, raising goosebumps on my skin. His aviator sunglasses matched nicely with his scowl. "You're not supposed to be here."

"It's a free country," Gabbi said.

I felt proud she actually stood up for herself, but messing with the police wasn't such a great idea. "We were just leaving. And your real problem is standing over there, probably spreading hepatitis or swine flu or HIV all over the street."

Officer Hanley looked, and then dropped his voice so low it was almost a whisper. Officer Hanley never whispered. "How long has he been there?"

Gabbi shrugged.

"Has he been in contact with anyone else?"

"What are you—" I said.

"Has he touched, or hurt, or otherwise injured anyone?"

"I don't think—"

"You need to leave this area. Now." He grabbed for his receiver and spoke some weird coded words, his voice clipped and fast.

I realized he was scared.

"You can't kick us off," Gabbi said. "We have a right—"

"Gabbi," I said. "We should listen to him." I pulled on her shirt. She took a resisting step back.

"You girls get out of here." The window began to close.

Gabbi yelled.

There was a loud bang.

We stumbled backwards as if skateboards had slipped out from under our feet. The creep had thrown himself against the backseat window of the cruiser. His hands smeared red down the glass and crushed whatever he had been holding, and then he dropped away as if knocked unconscious.

It wasn't a heart, I told myself, no matter how much it looked like a heart out of the books Gabbi and I had poured through together once at the library. Ricker had sworn he was having a heart attack at the ripe old age of thirteen—it had been heartburn but we hadn't known any different at the time.

A wild look came into Officer Hanley's eyes. He used his side mirror, then reached for the door handle.

A metallic voice barked from his dashboard. The words sounded like some sort of order. He returned both hands to the steering wheel. His gold wedding band glinted as he flexed his hands.

"You can't leave us here," I said.

He hesitated.

The creep hadn't stood up yet and that freaked me out. A lot. What if he was crawling around the car on all fours?

"Get in," Officer Hanley said.

A head appeared at the back bumper. The creep had been crawling.

I yanked open the passenger door, grabbed a handful of bills and coins from the jar, stuffed them in my pocket, pushed Gabbi into the front seat, and jumped practically on her lap. I slammed the door closed.

The grate kept Gabbi and me from crawling into the back seat. The window had a gap several inches wide. The creep's grimy, bloody fingers hooked through the gap, reaching for my hair. I couldn't breathe. Gabbi screamed.

"Do something!" I said, shrinking back.

"I have orders to lead him away," Officer Hanley said. "Don't let him touch you, don't let the blood get on you—you should have run."

"Story of my life!" I shouted.

The window rolled up enough to pin the creep's hands in place. The car moved forward several feet then settled into a slow, steady pace.

My stomach flipped. I stared at Officer Hanley because I couldn't stand looking at the creep's maniacal face any longer without going crazy myself. "You're going to, to...You should just shoot him!"

"Can't," Officer Hanley said. "Can't risk the blood." His forehead gleamed with sweat even though the air conditioning blasted frigid air. That was the only sign that maybe he wasn't feeling as cool as he acted.

It was like an insane form of dog walking. I looked everywhere but at the creep. The street was empty. Rush hour over, people inside. A couple of cars zipped by in the other direction, not even slowing. Up ahead was a four-way stop. A woman from the corner house dragged her garbage can to the gutter, saw us. Stopped. Stared. In a different house, a face appeared in the window, on a cell phone, also staring.

His fingers were dark red, bright red, grimed with mud and something slimy. He limped alongside the car, unseeing.

He twisted, pulled, pinched the glass, let it go. Something wet flew from his hands onto my face.

In my eye.

My eyelid closed on instinct. I flinched back into the seat. I blinked, rubbed at my eye, thought about all the terrible things probably infecting this meth head. I wiped my hand across my cheek. A small smear of blood transferred onto my skin. I wiped it off on my pants. I wanted to cry.

"What's wrong with him?" Gabbi said in a small voice. She'd wrapped her arms around my waist as if I could keep her from drowning.

"Drugs," I said. I told myself I'd gotten it off. It was fine. I was going to be fine. "He's high. Hopped up on a new meth recipe, right?"

Officer Hanley looked as if about to say something that would wreck my mind.

Sirens blared from everywhere. The inside of the car flooded with red and blue lights.

EVERYONE'S AN OOGLE AT FIRST

Posted August 10th at 6:46PM on Do More Than Survive: How to THRIVE as a Runaway

What my stepdad did to me, it made me stronger. People call me a miracle kid because of all the stuff I've already survived. People are always surprised at how happy I am about life still. Everything done to me has made me stronger.

He was doing cocaine—that was when I was, like, ten or something. My mom had me change my last name because they wanted to be a family or something. So I changed my name. I still have that name right now. It pisses me off because he would slam my head into the wall.

I don't think about it except you should know—I thought I knew everything to survive on the street since I'd pretty much been surviving on my own in that house for years already.

It doesn't matter how street smart you think you are. When you first become a street rat you're really just an oogle, which just means you're new to the street and stupid because you don't know the rules yet.

Until proven otherwise, other street kids are going to think you ran away from your trust fund, or because you think it's cool—basically, you're a poser. Accept it.

If you stay on the street long enough, you'll earn some street cred. But a tweeker never stays anything but an oogle.

I tell social workers I didn't run from my family, I ran to my family. But be careful about who you get help from. There are real sociopaths and murderers and abusers out there, those are the monsters you should worry about, not the ones the newspapers try to scare you about.

I'd say don't be an oogle, but you won't be able to help it. Learn from others—street kids stick together. There will always be someone willing to show you how things are done.

In the meantime, here are a few basic tips to get you started until you find your street family:

Stay clean. That's first. Clean hands, clean clothes. You're a dead giveaway and probably going to get the police or CPS called on you if you're dirty. There are water fountains, public restrooms at colleges and libraries, house hoses (watch out for dogs), water fountains, creeks (but watch out for pesticide runoff). No excuses.

If you're spanging, that's different. When you beg for money, it's important to show your customers a little dirt otherwise they won't feel good about giving you the cash. Also, spanging sucks. Everyone hates you, even those who give you money or food. It's the worst part, but it's the easiest and safest way to make some cash.

Thrift stores are good for changing into a cheap and clean set of clothes. Don't be a jerk—actually buy the clothes.

Get enough cash to buy a gym membership. Go in for a family plan with friends. Make sure and hold out for a great deal. For less than a $1 a day you can get access to bathrooms, hot water, showers, saunas, pools, and games 24/7 so you can stay clean and avoid getting picked up. This is my best tip because then you won't ever feel pressured to have sex with someone because they have a shower or a warm place to stay.

Get to know another runaway who has a car. Now you have a moving home and pretty good protection while you sleep. You can park the car in lots more places without being noticed than if you didn't have one. Plus it's nice being able to travel without watching the train schedules. You'll get to have favorite cities and favorite seasons in those cities. You'll stay in one place for a while and then just decide one morning to travel clear across the country to your other favorite city.

Don't blow all your cash on alcohol and drugs. I know a lot of you will, no matter what I say—even those of you who think that will never be them—because that's how me and my friends lived for a while. Just know that if you do, then you become trapped like all the 9-to-5 wage slaves you're supposed to be better than.

Don't ever feel like you'll worry about food. Americans waste so much food it's kinda evil. If you spend cash on food you're wasting your money. I'm a vegetarian and have never had any problems getting food I could eat, as long as I was staying in a city. It's called dumpster love. You'll see.

If you want to get picked up, or you're making a moral statement against consumerism, or you are sticking it to the world, then do the opposite of all the above.

But you better stay out of my way cause if you get me caught, me and my friends will come at you with smileys• and we won't feel bad about it for more than a minute.

•*For you oogles out there, a smiley is a weapon made out of a bike chain and duct tape, or a chain and a combo lock, or a bandana and a lock, or really anything close by that would hurt someone if you swung it at them.*

2

THE CREEP LAY FLAT ON the street, faceup. He twitched, stilled, twitched again. They'd stuck the creep with something that dropped him like a rock.

Every time he moved, I swear my eye flinched.

Two people in something like white moon suits hovered, taking measurements, writing on clipboards. People in navy jackets with yellow CDC lettering were erecting a tent around them.

Gabbi and I stood on the corner opposite the house of the woman and her trash can. The last direct rays of light turned the surrounding roofs a golden brown. The aroma of someone's backyard grill said a family was eating burgers like nothing had happened. A yellow line of tape hung between us and gawkers with their phones out recording every move. I kept our phone away. I wasn't like them, no matter how much I wanted to post about this. I wanted to help people who needed it, not enjoy someone's bad luck.

We were inside the taped circle. I very much wanted not to be. Officer Hanley had been nice to us before—sure he messed with our camps and kicked us off corners and out of squats, but he saved us even though we were street roaches.

Now he hovered feet away to make sure we couldn't leave.

I touched my eye and then forced my hand down. If I rubbed it anymore I was paranoid I'd break the skin.

Someone was going to call CPS. They'd act like they were doing it for my own good. They'd send me to a home, or ranch, or juvie. They'd tell me what to do, when to do it, how to do it—and have enough power to force me. I knew this. They had taken me in once. I had tried to kill myself.

"We've gotta get out of here," I said.

"No kidding," Gabbi said.

I was glad she had her courage back because at the moment I was like a little kid scared of the dark. I couldn't handle being trapped. She couldn't handle anything to do with her parents. We each had our traumas and tried to respect them.

I thought about how to get back to the van. I texted Ano a cryptic message about not coming after us. No sense them getting caught up in all this. They were at a nearby park, in a spot nestled among some old oaks we had claimed that day from the pervs that went to shag off together in the great outdoors. Otherwise the van was our home when we weren't at the library, the gym, the mall, or dreaming about owning our own piece of land one day.

The phone showed the second post had gone live. I was glad the information was getting out. I didn't know how to even begin to explain this situation, but I would find a way. I returned the phone to Gabbi's pocket.

A moon suit approached Officer Hanley. He motioned us over.

Moon suit held up a hand when we came within a few feet. "That's far enough." A woman's voice.

Her suit reeked of new rubber and plastic. This close, the clear plastic shield seemed to shrink her mouth and enlarge her eyes. Her glasses underneath were orange and made her blue eyes look like they were rimmed in fire. Her hair was stuck to her forehead, curled with pomade and pins.

"I am Dr. Ferrad. Please, understand time is of the essence. Were you scratched or bitten or otherwise injured?"

I didn't answer and so Gabbi remained silent too.

Office Hanley took a step forward but she held up her hand.

She raked her eyes over my legs, my bare collarbone, my arms, my face. Her face seemed larger than life behind the shield. She was the astronaut and we were the alien species she was deciding how to dissect.

Where the blood had landed on me felt like a neon sign. She must see it. She must know. And then she would take me away and they would never let me go.

Her eyes stopped on my arm. My arm of scars, naming all my dead street friends. The freshest was months old. A series of raised, whitish lines.

She passed by my eye like there was nothing special about it.

I released a long, slow breath.

She held up a finger, pointing at something on Gabbi's arm. "There."

It was a scratch. Long dried. "That's from this morning," I said. "The creep didn't do it." Gabbi had caught her arm on a jagged piece of metal. Standard stuff for us.

"Take them in," Dr. Ferrad said to Officer Hanley.

"It's not my fault," Gabbi said. "It's not from him."

Gabbi stepped back. Officer Hanley stepped forward. Dr. Ferrad set down the clipboard. The noise from the gawkers increased.

A groan rose above all the noise, then someone screamed.

The tent was only half up. The creep was sitting and had buried a pen into the arm of a white suit.

Dr. Ferrad yelled for Officer Hanley to watch the two of us before racing away.

Officer Hanley rested a hand on his holstered gun. "Stay where you are."

It seemed like all the navy jackets and uniforms had gotten sucked into the middle of the circle. Gawkers pressed into the yellow tape, holding up their phones, lights bright and blinding.

Energy rippled through the crowd. There were more screams, but this time from the crowd. A woman with a bloody face lurched into the tape and fell into Officer Hanley's arms.

People scattered.

I tugged on Gabbi's arm. "Time to go."

We ran.

Officer Hanley yelled our names, but the crowd hid us. People were pushing, tripping, screaming. Phones smashed to the ground. A shot fired, and then another, and another. Weird, muffled shots that sounded like whatever they'd dropped the creep with.

We sprinted across two lawns. A man wearing a red lumberjack kind of shirt appeared. I ran into him and lost my balance. He grabbed at me, his hands a dirty red. A metallic smell washed over me, making me want to wretch. His breath stank like something had died in there.

I punched the heel of my hand into the flesh of his neck. He curled his fingers into my clothing, pulling me closer. His face was crazy, cranked, like an axe murderer out of a movie.

My threadbare spanging shirt ripped. I fell onto the ground. He loomed over me like a demon shadow. A scream lodged in my throat. I scrambled up, scraping my palms, my knees. A fingernail peeled back, the pain striking up my arm like lightning.

Gabbi bowled into his side, knocking him over, but he sprung right back up.

We ran down the block. Our shoes slapped against the asphalt, our breaths turned ragged. My heart pumped a million times a second.

I looked back over my shoulder. Mr. Axe Murderer was running too, as if our sprint had only made him lock onto us like a predator giving chase. This guy was cranked just like the creep, but he sure didn't have a limp to hold him back.

Gabbi huffed behind me, but didn't cover the growls from the man running us down as if we were the last people on earth.

"What do we do?" Gabbi yelled.

I didn't answer because I didn't have an answer. She would do what I said as soon the words were out. For all her toughness and could-care-less act, there was no one in the group I trusted more than I trusted Gabbi, except maybe Leaf. But Gabbi was never any good with plans. She'd do something stupid, say something stupid. This was up to me to figure out, I just needed to come up with something, fast.

"Split up!" I yelled finally. "If he follows you, take the long way back to the van. If he follows me, get to Spencer and say it's like the station in Texas."

"What?" Gabbi's panicky voice cut off the end of the word.

"Just do it." I veered right. "Now!"

Gabbi followed me for a step, twisted, and sprinted in the other direction.

I waited to see who Mr. Axe Murderer would follow.

A few blocks away, it was still chaos, but it seemed like part of a television show. Screams, sirens, shots. All white noise to this meth head. A chill went up my spine. Meth heads were the worst. The most aggro. One guy had knocked out all of this other guy's teeth while we'd been train bound once in the Midwest.

Please let him just be a meth head.

He swiveled between me and Gabbi's disappearing form.

If he was going to follow anyone, it was going to me. I shouted and waved my hands around.

As if on cue, he tilted his head, sniffed, and then locked onto me.

A hiccup caught in my throat. This guy was going to catch me and eat me, and I would never see the others again or get to buy Jimmy his birthday present.

I willed my legs to work. I needed one of Gabbi's scathing remarks to belittle me into action. It was his teeth that finally made me move. His mouth hung open, showing off a bloody grin and split lip. The idea that he might eat me didn't seem so silly.

I ran for a gap behind the closest strip mall and raced around a pair of light blue dumpsters, toward a rusting gate that was always left unlocked. I'd pop through that into an empty lot cracked with weeds and broken glass. It backed up to the park. Gabbi would make it to the others. They'd be ready with our smileys. I just needed to bring him—

Someone had locked the gate.

Sweat poured down my back. The stench of cat piss flooded my nostrils.

A brand new, shiny padlock linked the two sagging sides together. It looked like a toy—unweathered, undented.

A grunt and snuffle sounded behind me.

I wished for Ano. I had lied. There was no one I trusted more than him, or the steel that entered into his eyes when he moved to stop someone from hurting somebody else—or take revenge on someone for having hurt somebody else. No one.

I whirled around.

Mr. Axe Murderer stretched out his hands like some sort of monster in a movie.

"You really need some new moves."

He stumbled as if my voice had tripped some sort of humanity switch. His throat produced a low growl of words too garbled to understand. If they were words at all. This guy was definitely on meth. Some new formula that really took it up a notch. I ignored the little voice in my head that asked—then what were the moon suits for?

"You don't have to do this."

He ground his teeth, making popping noises.

I scanned the dumpster, the gate, the lock, the broken glass and rat droppings, the few sticks of wood, scattered and splintered. There was only one way out.

I threw myself at the fence. It sagged and bent me back toward the ground. I pressed myself against the wire, which cut into my flesh, and started climbing.

Hands grabbed me around the ankles and pulled my feet off the fence. I hung stretched in the air, my fingers the only part keeping me from dropping. I kicked and twisted and fell back with a whoosh that knocked my breath away.

My feet found new toeholds. I reached the top bar, folded myself over, took a breath. I would flip over and drop to the ground and leave the creep behind.

The fence shook, almost throwing me off. A coin fell from my pocket, pinging the metal. The creep's face bobbed into view. He was climbing the fence. Crap.

I flipped like the top was a monkey bar and I was twelve years old showing my underwear off to the high school boys.

I dropped hard on my feet and pain shot up my shins. The rest of the coins spilled into the air, glinting copper and silver before disappearing in the weeds.

The creep dropped to the ground with a thump.

Shivers seized my muscles in spite of the heat.

There was something seriously wrong with this dude and it wasn't meth.

I raced through the broken glass and weeds, hopping over the low stone border that separated the lot from the park. Oak trees dotted the open field. The dirt was rock hard, the grass yellow and short from fire hazard mowing.

I leapt onto the dirt trail that bikers and pedestrians and horses used during the daylight hours. The sirens that had disappeared returned. I chanced a backward glance.

A flash from a cigarette lighter caught my eye. A figure stepped from the trees. Dark hair, almost black, trimmed and styled to look a little wild. A dark jean-colored shirt that almost matched his hair. Movie star lips and piercing eyes that hid everything inside.

Ano.

Gabbi had gotten to them in time. They were waiting. They were ready.

Ano looked past me. His eyes widened. He sprinted in my direction.

Something tripped my ankle. My leg twisted, lost traction. I slapped the ground like a fly swatter. My chin burst into waves of pain. Pain flared in my calf. Stars exploded before my eyes, but did not fully hide how the creep's mouth had latched onto my bare leg.

I punched the creep in the nose even before I could think. I had practice with that, waking up to someone on top of me and needing to react fast. I punched until his nose cracked like a stick. He de-latched. I slammed both hands against his ears. I dug a thumb into one eye and hooked my other thumb in his nose and pulled until the skin broke. Bile burned my throat, but I used my anger to push it down.

Then Ano came swinging his smiley.

A second later, the creep was unconscious next to me. There was now a gash along his temple and across his ear. Blood smeared his face like clown makeup, but it wasn't my blood—I didn't think it was my blood. I didn't want it to be my blood.

Sirens grew louder. Police cars and a dark van screeched to a halt at the park's edge.

Something grabbed my shoulders. I yelped.

"Let's go," Ano said over the impossibly loud sirens. "Get up. Get up."

"I can't," I said. "My ankle's twisted."

"It's not that bad."

"You don't have any idea how bad it is or isn't!"

Ano hooked his arms under me and lifted. "Come on." He pulled me into the bushes.

We crouched behind an oak tree in the bushes. Here in the brush it was dark and cool. The smell of blood was replaced by the smell of dried grass, sweet and papery. I felt my leg. There were dents. My fingers came away wet with blood and my entire leg felt like it was burning.

Yards away was the open field I had just run through, a winding trail, and an unconscious monster. Sirens turned off. Three navy jackets jumped out of the van. Two police officers set out rifles with scopes, a third came out with a dog.

Two horses trotted from the trees. The riders stared at the officers, not realizing how close Mr. Axe Murderer was. One horse spooked and reared up. The rider slipped onto the ground. The horse sprinted away. The other rider stopped her horse from bolting and veered back to her friend.

"Stop right there!" A man's voice said through a bullhorn. "Do not leave the area!"

Mr. Axe Murderer sat up and saw the woman on the ground. He went for her.

There was a crack, like a car backfiring.

His head exploded into red mist, spraying her face, neck, arms, shirt.

The mist cleared. People shouted from far away. The second horse bolted for the trees, the rider holding on to the mane.

"We are officers from California's Center for Disease Control. Remain where you are! We are here to help."

The horse did not slow. Another shot took it down, the thin, spindly legs twisting into the air, the woman disappearing underneath.

Ocean waves pounded in my ears. They weren't supposed to be using real bullets. They were supposed to be worried about the blood.

The navy jackets approached the field. The woods glowed orange and pink from the sunset, casting everything in this disturbing warm glow—as if instead of blood and guts and gore, people were meeting up for a picnic.

"Mary!" Ano whispered fiercely in my ear. "You're not helping!"

I came back as if from a dream and thought, this must be what shock feels like. I let go of his wrist. My fingernails had dug into his skin and drawn blood. I put my feet back under me.

Ano passed me, jumping around and then ahead of me so that I could follow. We twisted along the winding trail for another hundred yards, deep into the darkening woodland, deep into the tall, dry grasses no one had bothered to mow because it was too far in to care about. The grasses scratched against each other and against us, making noise louder than the shouts behind us. I ignored the pain in my leg.

Ano veered at a downed tree. We burst into a small cleared area. On this side of the park, ranch houses and acres of horse property rimmed the border. Holdovers from before this place had become big enough to be called a city.

Our van was there and Jimmy was in the passenger seat, waving. Leaf held open the van door.

Once inside, it took long seconds for my eyes to adjust.

Everyone was there. Gabbi and Ricker in the back with me, Ano and Leaf and Jimmy. Spencer sat in the driver's seat. He was so tall his brown hair brushed the ceiling sometimes. People thought he was in his twenties even though he was only nineteen. He'd left home at fourteen, not because anything was really wrong at home but because he'd gotten tired of the shouting.

"Burn some rubber," Leaf said. "But be careful, that left back tire has a thin tread." Leaf could have been a football player if he'd stayed in school. He had the build and the looks, with his wide-set eyes, curly, messy, light brown hair, a cleft chin. He always scrunched his nose when he smiled.

"I remember." Spencer gunned the engine, rocking the cab.

I lifted myself onto a bench seat and the others did likewise. I took in a deep, slow breath. Hints of the lavender-scented shampoo we all used from the fitness center filled my nose. So did our sweat from spending a hot summer day on the street. None of us ever seemed completely able to wash it off.

It all smelled like home.

Jimmy turned around and stared at me. "Are you okay?"

"Happy birthday, Jimmy," I said, grinning, but the look on his face told me it must have come out as more of a grimace.

Ricker laughed. Leaf smiled. I couldn't see Gabbi's face but I suspected she would be frowning. Spencer didn't smile either. I didn't look for Ano's expression in case I burst into tears.

I pulled out a fistful of bills from my pocket. No coins were left. An oncoming car's headlights lit up the faces of my friends. "Hot showers, anyone?"

"Yes, please," Gabbi said.

Ano broke open the first aid kit we kept stashed under the front seat. Leaf rummaged through the clothes cabinet.

At the next light, Ano set himself up on the floor of the van and began to look me over. The disinfectant stung, but I gritted my teeth. He handled my ankle like it was fragile glass that might shatter. Too late, I wanted to tell him. I'd already been shattered and put myself back together. But that really could have described any of us.

He dabbed a rag at the bite.

"Pour the whole bottle on it," I said to Ano, wishing I could use it on my eye too.

Leaf pulled out an oversized lavender sweatshirt and a pair of threadbare, royal purple sweat pants and tossed them to me.

"Gee, thanks."

Leaf ignored my sarcasm. "What happened after you and Gabbi split up?"

I explained about Mr. Axe Murderer and the lock. "How does it look?" I said.

"You'll live," Ano said.

"Unless I'm infected with whatever that creep had," I said quietly.

He rested a hand on my bare knee and I lost myself in the dark pools of his eyes.

"You'll be fine," Gabbi interjected.

I smiled, the moment interrupted. Her grimace only deepened because she knew I was faking it for her sake. She wasn't stupid, just sometimes seemed that way because she was so stubborn.

"We should take her to the emergency room," Ricker said, always the practical one. He wanted to get off the street and maybe become a bus driver one day. He thought maybe he'd like helping people travel around.

"If we take her," Spencer said, "Then they'll take her. She'll be deep in the system and might never come back out."

Ricker pressed his lips together in a grim line. The chug of the engine changed to a low whine as Spencer turned into a parking lot. Spencer knew more about the system than any of us. He was the only one who had finished high school so far, on account of his being locked up and forced to do it. If you really wanted to get Spencer mad, you asked him about school.

"What do you want to do?" Ano said.

Everyone seemed to wait for my answer. I didn't know what the right answer was, only what I wanted most at that moment. "I just want to take a shower."

The van stopped. "We're here," Spencer said.

Through the front windshield, the fitness club sign glowed red against the pink sky. Inside there were hot showers, running water, real bathrooms available at any time of day. No one could kick us out as long as we paid our dues. We'd started the contract through a gift debit card Spencer had picked up at the liquor store. As long as we kept it on file, we could pay cash on the account.

Leaf pulled out an envelope from the clothes cabinet. He held out his hand for the dollars in mine.

"I usually pay. He expects me to pay," I said.

"He's going to have to take a rain-check," Ano said, because everyone knew how I paid our dues when we were short sometimes.

I looked over my bloody clothes and gave over the green.

Leaf jumped out. "I'll be back in a sec."

Ano closed the door and held up the purple clothes. "Put this over what you're wearing. We can't get you inside looking like that." He grabbed a rag and a gallon milk jug we stored water in. He soaked the rag and then started scrubbing at my face.

"Ow," I said.

"You look like you murdered someone," Ano said.

"I know," I said. "Kind of feels like it."

"How would you know?" Ano said.

"May I never know."

Ano worked away at my forehead, then my neck.

"Gabbi," I said. "Do you have the phone?"

She pulled it out and handed it to me. I opened the message app and began typing.

"What are you doing," Ano said quietly.

"I don't know how to put what's happening right now in words, but there's a lot of other stuff I have to say."

"You can do it later. We should be focused on cleaning up and leaving town."

I shook my head. I didn't know how to explain that there was this sinking feeling inside me. It said I probably didn't have much time left. Street kids felt that way a lot. I had felt that way before and I was still alive. But this seemed different somehow.

"If I don't get this out there now. I feel like, I don't know, I feel like it's going to drain out of my brain and I'll never remember it."

He shook his head, his dark eyes disappearing in the growing shadows. "You always remember when it matters."

I stopped, then reached for his hand and held it. "Maybe not this time." In spite of the heat, he shivered.

"Stop it, Mary," Gabbi said. "Don't talk like that."

"All right, Gabbi. Sorry." I swallowed around a lump forming in my throat. "So…you and me, we should go spanging again tomorrow, don't you think? We've got to take advantage of our lucky streak while it lasts."

"Oh shut up," she said, but there was a smile in her words.

To be honest, I felt a hint of a smile on my lips because this was the part I liked best—lifting people's spirits when things were really crappy. "There was this one dude today," I said, "he got all up in our business when he saw the phone, but we set him straight."

"You almost pushed him into the street!" Gabbi said.

"You would have, if I hadn't done it," I said.

"Yeah, thanks, but no, I wouldn't have."

"You would have if he'd been picking on me," I said.

"But he went for Gabbi," Ano said. "And you didn't let him."

"She just stood up," Gabbi said, standing up and reenacting the scene, "and he was like head and shoulders taller than her, but he wouldn't stop messing with us, so she got up between me and him, and it doesn't even matter that he's all red in the face and about to call the cops. She pushed him twice until he got a clue." Gabbi laughed. "He pretty much ran down the block after that."

"See," Ano said, caressing the back of my hand with his thumb. "You remember what to do when it counts."

The quick adrenaline rush of the retelling drifted away. "Yeah. I guess so."

I finished the blog post while he finished scraping my face with the rag. There was a lot more I had planned to say, but I couldn't remember it at the moment. I saved it as a draft so I could finish it later. I hoped Ano was right—that this time was like all the others and I'd figure out a way to survive it.

I tapped the button and returned the phone to Gabbi's care. I realized Jimmy hadn't said a word for a long time. "Jimmy? Are you okay?"

A sniffling sound came from his direction.

"It's going to be okay, Jimmy," I said.

Spencer looked away. So did Ricker, Ano, Gabbi. No one wanted to make him feel bad for crying. We all cried sometimes. We all did our best to hide it.

The metal rollers screeched as the door opened. Leaf stood in semi-shadow, the sign lights casting an eerie neon line around his body. He was only fifteen, but had been a throwaway for two years. One day he told his mom he was gay and she told him never to come back.

The parking lot was empty, the sky now a dull imitation of its earlier colors. Leaf looked at Spencer and something passed between them that none of us could read. They did that sometimes. They'd been together for awhile now.

"We're good."

▪

Steam filled the bathroom with curtains of damp air. The tile was slippery, cold, welcoming. Female voices bounced off the ceramic walls and created a sort of chaotic foundation of noise that soothed me. Gabbi and I stepped into different stalls, having left the boys to their side of the bathrooms.

I blasted the shower on full and let the lavender shampoo and hot water wash away the sweat, the blood, the dirt. The pain of the heat mixed with the pain in my leg. The wound was fiery, red, puckered. But it was my eye that burned like a black widow bite, the poison creeping through my skin and muscles, entering my blood stream, poisoning my system along the way. The leg bite had only added insult to injury. I told myself if I wasn't feeling better in two hours I would make them dump me at the closest hospital.

The water drummed on my back like the rhythm of a train on the tracks. Hopping a train was always a rush. Like when you get your first tattoo. That kind of rush. It's like the best movie screen. You just sit there and maybe you're high or drunk, or not, it doesn't matter. You see these places, these dark forests and blue-black nights and stars and mountains and there is no other way to see them.

The water cut off with a whine and a trickle.

I dried myself off with a towel, scrubbing my skin until it flushed red, breathing in the clean scent of the cotton. Blood trickled in two rivulets down either side of my ankle. The flesh had swelled enough I thought the bite would stop bleeding soon.

I tied a strip of cloth tight around my calf and dressed in the purple outfit I was still stuck with.

Our phone rested on the bench next to Gabbi's clothes. I sat down with it and texted out everything I could think of about how to run away and keep from making my same mistakes. The post felt jumbled, unconnected, but I felt better when it was all down.

I decided to make it go live, right then. Just in case.

The app's progress bar moved, then stalled. I stared at it, willing the bar to move just a little more, but there wasn't enough signal. An error message popped up and said it would try again every five minutes until it completed the connection. That would have to do.

I locked the phone and waited for Gabbi and thought about what to do next.

We were all together now, we had been together, watching out for each other for years. We could rely on one another to get out of scrapes and mistakes and danger. We had plans to get off the streets and then we'd be safe for good and no one would stop us. We'd get out of town and then visit some random med clinic. I'd tell them a homeless guy had bitten me and they would pump me so full of antibiotics I'd have the runs for weeks.

End of infection. End of a crazy story I would then write about for days, but only as fiction. Otherwise no one would believe it.

Four women entered the bathroom, their voices sharp and loud and full of derision. One of the women looked at me, just looked at me. She wore yoga pants and a tight-fitting tank top, black on bottom, bright pink on top. Her face said she knew I didn't belong there. Two of the women dropped used towels on the tile floor and kept walking. The pitch of their voices slapped the walls and then my ears. My head flared with pain and red washed over my vision.

She spoke even though her mouth didn't open. She looked right at me and said, "You're a whore and your mother is a whore and no wonder your stepdad beat you. Leave now while you still have the chance."

I curled my fists and a low growl crept into my throat. How dare she. I paid my dues. We paid and we didn't come in here acting like we owned the place, acting like we could do whatever we wanted, dropping towels on the ground for someone else to pick up.

"Mary?"

I whirled, readying a punch.

Gabbi's eyes widened and she raised her hands to block a blow. Her hair rested in wet tendrils around her shoulders, dampening her shirt.

But I would never hit her.

Conversation stopped. The silence deafened me.

I realized the woman hadn't said a word to me. I'd imagined it, but it had seemed so real.

I opened my hands and forced my arms to my sides. The sound of shower water filled the space.

Gabbi glared at the women. They looked away. "Come on. Let's go."

We went from the shower stalls to the locker area. Side by side, like I hadn't been about to attack her. The women laughed at something, probably us.

"Did they ask for your ID, too?" One of the women said, her words almost lost in the way it slapped around the tile.

We both froze.

"Right after class. They aren't letting anyone out until they check your ID."

"Did they say who they're looking for? What would they be doing here?"

"Lots of weird stuff in the news these days. I'm just glad I got my mother-in-law to take the kids for an hour. I can't bother to keep up with much else."

Gabbi grabbed my sleeve. I walked to the bathroom entrance and looked out. The cool air conditioning was a shock after the humidity of the bathroom. The suits had arrived. One currently waited outside rooms opposite from us. Two more moved around treadmills and weight benches, pausing to look at faces and then moving on.

"How did they know we were here?" I said.

"Does it matter?" Gabbi said.

We shrunk into the shadow of the bathroom entrance. I pressed myself into the stone wall and looked back into the women's bathroom, and then out to the men hunting for us. "I'll get the boys."

"Mary," Gabbi hissed.

I slipped across the open space separating the two sides. The humidity hit me like a wet blanket. A young guy sat on the bench, toweling his hair, another small white towel around his waist. He looked up and raised an eyebrow at me.

I smiled and said, "Sorry, just looking for my friends."

"It's all right." He smiled back.

"Spencer!" I shouted loud enough for them to hear but not loud enough to draw attention from outside. "Food's getting cold!" Which was our fancy secret code for it was time to get the hell out.

The boys tumbled out of the shower area in various states of dress and wetness, but done up enough to go in public. Ano looked good dressed in loose pants and bare chest that showed off his tan and dozens of white scars.

I didn't say anything, just forced a smile at Spencer's look so he would know we were in real trouble.

Leaf grabbed a pile of stuff from the bench and headed past me out of the bathroom. I turned to walk alongside him.

"Bad?" he said.

"Not good," I said.

"How's the leg?"

"Not so good either."

He wrapped an arm around my shoulders. For a moment, a half breath, a millisecond, this spark lit up inside of me, it told me to hurt him because he wasn't allowed to touch me without asking, and I would teach him a lesson so that he would never, ever touch anyone again.

Bile stung my throat. I pushed myself away and walked into the center of the main workout space, veering for one of the suits.

Leaf was the kindest, gentlest, most brotherly person of all the people I had ever, ever known. He would never hurt me, he was only offering the comfort I had often sought out from him. What was wrong with me?

My stomach twisted. Pain flared in my calf. I stumbled, knee touching the cushioned floor. I looked up and locked stares with one of the suits.

"Hey." He stretched out his arm. "Stay where you are." He pulled out a phone and spoke into it.

The two other suits turned like robots. I felt their gaze on me, evaluating me, undressing me. I would make them pay. I would—

"Mary!" Gabbi hissed. She grabbed me on one side, and suddenly Ano was there and he lifted me off the ground.

The fire alarm went off. The ringing covered the dance music. A strobe light flashed. People streamed from the rooms, the treadmills, the pools. The women rushed out of the bathroom.

The suits yelled and waved their hands and pushed people aside, but no one heard them over the alarm. Their pushing only made people freak out more.

A family of five ran for the front doors, two women followed, and the chaos grew and bottlenecked at the people-counter. The suits tried to stop the tide. An older man must have been shouting because his face turned purple.

Finally the suits stood back and opened the door. The alarm continued its piercing tone. A middle-aged woman slapped her hands over her ears. Two teenagers tried their headphones.

Gabbi and Ano helped me hop over the people-counter next to a bodybuilder still slick with sweat and oil. The suits couldn't see us.

A dark van and cop car, sirens and lights off, were parked next to our van. The doors were open, shadows were inside. One of them stepped outside, into the parking lot light. Officer Hanley. Even in the chaos, he saw us, shouted, pointed. The other uniforms jumped out.

Ano said, "Around then. Quick."

It seemed like everyone inside the gym was now outside. People milling around, phones out, asking others what was happening. I waited for the groan and growl of a monster to start up. It was too close to what Gabbi and I had just been through. Crowds were bad news.

Spencer pushed people away and made a path. We rounded the corner. The crowd closed behind us, creating an obstacle course for the uniforms. The alarm faded into a dull ringing.

Leaf took the lead, making us run behind the dumpsters, through an alleyway, out back behind a grocery store we scored leftover fruit from on Wednesdays.

We continued silently on foot. Leaf stopped at the next block, a strip mall where people only ordered dinner for take out, never dine in. The greasy smells drifting out of the Chinese hole-in-the-wall made my stomach rumble with hunger and a sudden queasiness. I hadn't eaten since early that morning. A cash advance place had closed for the night, though the entire inside was still lit up and the sign glowed a nauseous green.

"I did it," Jimmy said. "I pulled the fire alarm. I did just like you said, Spencer. I really did it." His voice raised in pitch.

Ano let go of me and I was suddenly drifting. The building, the lights, the trees, the people, it all wavered, just a little bit. Jimmy shouldn't be talking so loud. He was going to get us found. We were a bunch of teenagers who looked like they'd just run away from a bunch of trouble. He needed to shut up.

"Mary, what are you doing?" Ano's voice came from far away. All I could see was Jimmy's pinched, young face. Flushed from the run, from the showers, from the pride of pulling the alarm that had kept me from turning myself over to the uniforms and saving them all. It was his fault.

"Get away, Mary, just back off!" Ano jumped between me and Jimmy.

I stopped. I didn't understand why I had stopped. Why had I been moving? Why were my hands in the air, my fingers curled into claws?

I stood there, swaying on my feet, trying to figure this out. It was ME, I was the one who jumped between oogles and trouble. I was the one, not him, not anyone else. Why was he standing there, looking at me like that?

HOW TO PREPARE

Posted August 10th at 7:46PM on Do More Than Survive: How to THRIVE as a Runaway

Practice running away before you actually run away. Pretend you're going to sleep over at a friend's house for a day or two and then go sleep out in the woods, eat out of some dumpsters, use only public restrooms to wash up.

Also, put good karma out into the world and leave a note to whoever you left behind—whether or not you think they care about you. I called my mom after I left. She said she was worried about me out here, but not enough to leave my stepfather. But I called, and I was even nice about it, plus, then you won't get reported as a kidnapping. Let the police spend time and money on finding kids who want to go home. Remember, no one likes a jerk.

Figure out what you're going to do with all the extra time once you run away. Other kids your age are going to be in school. Unless you get involved in drugs, or alcohol, or prostitution—not recommended unless you ran away because you secretly want to kill yourself, which was what I wanted at first —you are going to have a lot of free time on your hands.

This is important because at some point you're gonna rest your head on your pillow and know that you are sleeping on concrete and you're gonna start crying. Don't let anybody see it cause it'll make you a target. But it will happen. You'll get so upset about your life and realize that you maybe wished you'd finished the school year or gone to the school swim party at least once, just to know what it would have been like.

This is when your goal or dream or wish becomes really important to your survival because otherwise there's no point getting up the next day except for the alcohol and drugs.

Every street kid has one. What's yours going to be? Maybe right now, it's only to get out, to get some adventure, to get free of whatever beatings your stepdad did every night.

Okay, but now you're out, so now what?

Me and my friends, we have a plan. We're going to save up enough money to buy some land, we're thinking maybe in Arizona where it's cheap and warm. Or maybe in the State of Jefferson, in the woods with other people who understand that society has it all wrong. It's going to be our own place. We'll grow a garden and brew our own beer and live together and no one can kick us off it just for breathing because we'll own it.

3

"We have to run," Gabbi said.

"I know," Spencer said.

"We have to get out of here. People are going to notice," she said.

"I know," Spencer said.

I sat hunched over on the curb. I'd puked my guts out after Ano had stopped me from choking Jimmy.

Jimmy hovered on the far side of the group now, next to Spencer. They talked over me as if I wasn't even there.

Gabbi opened her mouth again.

Spencer held up his hand. "Gabbi, I know it. Just hold on."

She closed her mouth and crossed her arms.

"If they knew we were going to be at the fitness center—how did they know?" Leaf said.

“They didn’t,” Spencer said. “Officer Hanley knows where most of our regular haunts are. He got lucky we were at the one he checked out.”

“What are we going to do about Mary?” Ricker said.

“She’s fine,” Gabbi said.

“She’s not fine,” Ricker responded.

“I am,” I said.

“You are not,” Ricker said.

“I was chased, almost taken prisoner, beaten up,” I said, my throat croaking from the stomach acid that had burned it. “I think that would make anyone a little wacko. God knows you’ve had your moments, Ricker. Do you need me to remind you?”

Ricker ignored my jab. “What about the puking? What about Jimmy?”

“I’ve done more running in the last three hours than in the last three weeks. So I puked. It feels better now. I got angry at Jimmy. Not at Jimmy. I just got angry, and he was there.”

“You don’t get angry,” Gabbi said.

“Yes she does,” Spencer said quietly. “She used to.”

Ano sat next to me and pulled me to his side. I leaned into him and didn’t care that everyone noticed Ano and I were having a moment.

“Mary,” Leaf said, a warning note in his voice.

Six pairs of eyes turned on me as if I had already been convicted of murder. “What?”

“Your mouth,” Ricker said. “There’s white, leftover puke or something—”

I swept my hand across and felt something wet, like I’d drooled in my sleep. For a long second I could only think about choking and didn't know if I was about to choke myself or them. Them, me. It almost didn't matter.

"I want to get out of town. That's all I want," I said. "Get me out of town and drop me off at a clinic. But not here. Please. Not here."

Ricker looked to Spencer and Leaf. They were the unspoken leaders, especially when I was down for the count. The van was a tough loss, our extra clothes, basic supplies, a fast way out of town, all gone. But it was only stuff. This wasn't the first time it had happened. Though I suspected it would take more than a simple impound fee to get it back this time.

Spencer raised an eyebrow. Leaf nodded in assent. Somehow they had decided, even though they hadn't spoken a word to each other.

I should have been able to guess that decision, would have normally helped make it, but couldn't think what it should be at that moment. Ano pressed his chin against my hair. I decided I would enjoy that feeling instead of worrying about things I couldn't control.

"We might have lost the van," Leaf said, "but there's still the bikes."

"But you just said they'll be checking out all our normal haunts," Ricker said. "We need to hitchhike or catch a bus or jump a train."

"The bikes are on the way to the trains," Spencer said. "If we get to them, we get out of town faster, maybe get some info."

"If they're hot?" Ricker said.

"Then we'll keep going, idiot," Spencer said.

Spencer broke us up into groups. Gabbi, me and Ano in one. Spencer and the rest in the other. They didn't dare leave Jimmy with me and this made me want to cry. But they were right to do it. Ano and Gabbi could handle the worst in me, if it came to that. We'd done it for each other often enough. This was one of those hard times that sometimes happened on the street. They would know what to do.

We took the back streets, the side roads, the empty lots, the alleys, the parking lots, the open fields. We hurried onto the bike trail, our preferred way to get from one side of the city to the other when public transportation wasn't running. It was easy, flat, beautiful, and nobody yelled at us to get out. We could pop into dozens of neighborhoods from it.

The cooler air rising off the river washed over me, smooth, refreshing, soothing my thoughts and emotions. The air smelled muckier here, but still cleaner than the streets. The sun had long disappeared over the horizon, all the colors gone, leaving only gray light behind. Vines climbed the oak trees that lined the river. Open spots revealed fields of yellow grass cropped short for fire control. We weren't that far from the bike shop now, but we had to walk it and I had a limp.

I asked Gabbi for the phone and typed out another post as we went. It didn't take me long because there wasn't much left to say. I used to burst with things to write, and now this little message seemed so hard.

"If anyone shows up," Gabbi said, "there aren't a lot of hiding places on the trail."

Her words interrupted my momentary focus. The trauma of the day crowded back in. I wished she hadn't said that. "There's the bushes," I said. "The trees, the grass on that side. We could cross the damn river if we had to." My voice rose at the end. My head started pounding, like someone was knocking my skull against a wall. I closed my eyes and saw red, bright, fire-engine red. A whole wall of it and my head banged against it.

"Mary?" Gabbi's voice from far away.

"Maybe Ricker is right," Ano said.

The thought of being left behind, dumped off at the emergency room for the moon suits to find me while they all got out of town, this took the rest of my stomach. I vomited saliva onto the bike trail.

I wiped my mouth on my arm, and then tapped to publish the post in an hour. It was my last little act of hope—maybe things would turn out all right and I could delete it before it went live.

The two of them stood back a few feet, looking in different directions as if keeping watch, or not wanting to look, probably both.

"I'm better now," I said. "Don't dump me."

Ano flinched.

"That's not going to happen," Gabbi said. She took the phone I offered.

I waited for Ano to say something. He looked down the trail as if he could see a thousand miles away. "Do you need help walking?"

I imagined one of them touching me, helping me, and feared it might cause an explosion. "I'm okay," I said. "Really. Throwing up helped." I had always made it a point never to lie to them, but that was a lie.

I used all my strength to step down the trail again. We paused at the incline that would take us from river level up and over the levee wall. I thought maybe if I stayed still and closed my eyes for a moment the pain in my head would lessen.

It didn't.

I forced one step over the other. A hand reached out to grab my elbow, as if to steady me.

I snarled. "Don't touch me."

The hand disappeared as if bitten by a snake.

I made it up the twenty-foot mountain and paused at the top, breathing hard, this time with my eyes open because it hadn't done any good to keep them closed. The winding levee road disappeared between the trees, and everything was gray, gray, gray. The brilliant sunset that would have cast a pink glow on the river water, the clouds, the trees, the faces of Gabbi and Ano as they waited to see what I would do next—long gone.

I wanted to curl up and burst into tears and tell them to please take the pain in my head away and take away my upset stomach and maybe it would have been nice to finish high school at least. I think I would have liked to go to prom once. Just to see.

"Wait here," Gabbi said finally, she dug the toe of her shoe into the gravel, disturbing a line of black ants. "I'll get the bikes."

"No," I said, finding my voice, shaking my head to clear it a little. I wondered if I had any more spittle on my lips but I was too tired to check. "I'll go." I was dangerous and they needed to leave me behind. They'd understand that eventually. Plus it would be nice to see Ike one more time. He'd always allowed us to change our flat tires, and effortlessly argued with me about prices and borrowing tools from his shop in order for Ano and Gabbi to modify the bikes the way we wanted—a cross between utilitarian practicality and Mad Max flare—fixies, because brakes and gear shifts always failed, streamers and bells and trick bars, because being runaways didn't mean we lost our sense of style.

We entered the neighborhood of ranch-style houses with big front yards and double garages and lawn furniture that cost more than Spencer's van was worth. The shop was one block in. The sign on the front, Ike's Bikes, was faded wood with red lettering and a red border. A little hole-in-the-wall where bikes filled the space from floor to ceiling, requiring you to bend around tires hanging at face level. Ike also had an inventory building in the back almost as big as the store, with a mini-kitchen and a bathroom that he allowed us to use sometimes.

Ike was out front, smoking, almost like he was waiting for someone.

"Just stay here," I said.

Gabbi squatted onto the ground, against a redwood tree's trunk so large the three of us couldn't hold our hands around it. The bushes were thick here, against the edge of someone's property, obscuring us from the bike shop, but providing a clear line of sight. Ano remained standing. It didn't matter what I said, he would follow whether I liked it or not.

I stepped into the street.

Someone in a navy jacket with that bright CDC lettering stepped around the corner of Ike's Bikes.

I lost my nerve and crouched behind a bush. The two of them spoke. Ike stubbed out his cigarette and went back inside. Navy jacket went around back.

Gabbi sucked in her breath. "We're not getting our bikes today. Where's Spencer and the others?"

"It doesn't matter," Ano said. "If they are caught, they are caught. If they are not, we should move and catch up to them."

"But where are they?" Gabbi said.

"On their way to the trains," I said. I told myself to stand up and walk across the street and around the shop and turn myself in. I didn't move. The air blurred into wavy lines. Gabbi sidled across the dirt and crouched next to me. Heat came off her body in waves. Reddish waves that pounded into me and wouldn't stop. She needed to back off. She needed to stop throwing this heat at me like a weapon, didn't she know I could stand up for myself now? I wasn't going to take it, I just wasn't, I just wasn't anymore—

▪

A rumble started deep in my chest and moved into my legs and arms and head. The pain woke me up. The relentless, pounding pain in my head that made me feel like someone was bouncing my skull off a wall.

I opened my eyes and saw people. The backs of people. Sitting two by two, in plaids, solids, tanks and t-shirts. I sat up. My head had been bouncing off a glass wall.

The window of a bus.

Through the bus mirror, I noticed the driver was an older lady, in her fifties, plump, gray-haired, hawkish eyes and a frown permanently set into her sagging skin. She caught my eye and I looked away, not wanting to be noticed, because getting noticed would surely get us into more trouble.

Gabbi sat at the aisle, cradling her hand in her lap. Ano sat next to me. There was a peacefulness to the hum of the engine, the rhythm of the tires, the shake of the bus. I should tell him. I should tell him and then he would help me figure this all out and maybe we could really belong to each other.

I reached for Ano's hand. He froze as if I were a monster about to attack. I grabbed his hand anyway. When nothing bad happened, he relaxed and squeezed back.

Gabbi shifted. As if in slow motion, a drop of bright red liquid splashed to the metal floor.

I dropped Ano's hand. "What did I do?" I carefully pushed out the words because the act of talking caused my throat a great deal of pain.

Gabbi didn't answer for a long moment. When she did she didn't look at me. "You passed out."

"Why are you holding your hand?"

This time she glanced at me, but still she hesitated. Gabbi wasn't one to hesitate. She was one to act rashly, to speak her mind, however cruelly, to confront a person with the brutally honest truth of their stupidity.

My stomach began acting up on me again.

"We told the bus driver you were drunk and we were getting you home safe."

I grabbed for her hand and she flinched.

She flinched like Ano had.

I drew back as if I'd touched a hot stove. I locked my fingers together in my lap. Ano stared wide-eyed back and forth between the two of us.

"Show me," I said.

Gabbi shook her head.

"Show her," Ano said.

She separated her hands and peeled back a piece of cloth I realized had been torn from the bottom of her shirt.

On the backside of her right hand were bite marks, most shallow enough to have only created bruising, several deep enough that they wept blood.

She covered the wound back up. "It's not a big deal. We all flip out sometimes."

A roar of air rushed to my ears. I had done this thing to Gabbi. I had bitten her and I couldn't even remember doing it. And now Gabbi, fearless Gabbi, the one who had never been scared, not after that one night in the Florida squat, after we had met her and taken her in and showed her how the world worked, now she had the same look on her face as that first night. That same look of helplessness.

And I had put it there.

"Ano?" I said.

"This is our stop," he said, talking to the window.

The bus slowed, everyone leaned forward. The air pistons released and the bus doors swung open with a jerk as the hydraulics lowered it several inches closer to the ground.

Ano helped me up, except he avoided using his left arm, and so I knew. I had injured both of them and couldn't remember any of it.

"It's going to be okay," Ano said, but his eyes revealed the lie in his words.

The passengers stared at us, at me, even though no one actually looked. It was like they were purposely not looking, like when I'd first run away and was dirty and alone on an East Coast subway, not caring where I was going as long as it was away from that house, from all of that anger, from all of that violence, and I had vowed I would never become a monster who hurt the people I cared most about.

The bus sped away into the dark, the exhaust fumes tasting like poison on my tongue. The curb felt unsteady beneath my shoes, as if I were on an elevator that had dropped out from beneath me.

Conversations echoed off the mansion-like interior of the train station. Murals, stained glass and architecture from a long time ago alongside plastic-molded benches and bright monitor screens showing arrival and departure times. And then the smells took over—of people, of unwashed human bodies, of perfumes and colognes and deodorants, of shampoo and hairspray, of lotion and toothpaste.

I couldn't hop the train. I wouldn't. I was sick. I was hurting my friends. I was every dangerous thing to them I had once warned them about.

And then I smelled lavender shampoo. I smelled them—my friends. Spencer and Ricker and Leaf and Jimmy.

My body pinged as if sparked by electricity. Every cell in me lit on fire with the desire to find them and—

I sprinted across the tile floor and out through the back exit. I sniffed the air, following their familiar scent of street sweat and fitness center shampoo. I followed the trail around the building. The back of my mind cataloged the scene—how Ano tried to hold me back, how Gabbi hovered, how several dark vans were parked in a line along the curb, how people trailed like ants from the station to the platforms, how a departing train whistled as it chugged along, slow at first and then picking up speed until it turned into a moving missile.

There.

Tucked against the back corner of a shed that stored tools and machinery. My friends were dark shadows against the outside of the tin wall that glinted orange from the outdoor lights. They were waiting for us.

A keening started in my throat. My mouth filled with saliva. I ran faster.

▪

The wall, the ground, the trains in the background, the lights that should have been orange, my friends huddling together while backing away from me, arms outstretched as if to ward me off—everything had turned red.

Ricker from the shoulder. Jimmy from the hand. Spencer and Leaf from the arms. Ano now from both his leg and arm.

I fell to my knees and puked, and then kept puking when I saw the red flecks and white flesh in the first pile.

Strings of pink saliva hung from my lips to the ground like spaghetti noodles. Tears leaked out of my eyes. I tried to say I was sorry but only groaned.

Ano used his soothing voice, the one he only brought out when he was talking down a scared, cornered dog, but his voice was too low for me to understand. He stepped toward me.

Spencer said something sharp.

I held up my hand. Don't come near me. Stay away.

Ano took another step. Rivulets of blood traveled down his arm and dripped from his elbow onto the ground.

I crawled away and huddled against the wall. And then I smelled it—new rubber and plastic and pomade and found the courage too late.

I sprang up, scaring Ano back a few steps.

"Mary?" he said, an ache in his voice.

I ran from them.

The vans were still parked on the curb, and two suits spilled out of the back right then, not noticing me. I willed myself to stop, willed myself not to lose it again.

I forced my feet to slow down, dropped to my knees. I waited for them to notice me.

When they did, everything became action and noise and dizziness. People appeared in those blazing white moon suits, covered head to toe, with a transparent mask. They held out a pole with a loop around the end of it. A dog catcher pole with a slip knot.

The noose settled on my shoulders and then tightened around my neck. My body shuddered. I wanted to fling myself at their throats and bury my mouth into the soft flesh between the shoulder and neck. The pain of holding myself back threatened to make me black out.

I spit out a glob of mucus and blood and who knows what else—parts of my friends. I didn't know if I could talk anymore, didn't know if there were any words left in me.

"Please help," I croaked.

The slip knot tugged at my neck. Get up, the pole told me.

I rose and staggered forward until the pole brought me up short. The white suit led me into a white tent. The flaps billowed and covered my vision in white like everything had been washed clean.

"Your name is Mary, right? Hello, Mary, can you hear me?" The helmet obscured the face, and the voice was ambiguous but familiar somehow. My head lolled to the side and everything in the tent tilted. The tent walls, the tray of medical tools, the IV pole and bag with a line inserted into my left arm. I realized there were two moon suits in the room. The one talking and another one standing just inside the tent door, arms at the sides, legs slightly bent, as if ready to tackle anything in the room that moved.

I couldn't remember how or when the IV got there. Only that they had used the noose to place me in a chair, and then had strapped me down at the neck, wrists and ankles.

"Mary, can you hear me? Nod your head. Or, if that's too difficult, blink twice to let me know."

I nodded, even though my neck felt swollen and hot and my skull was top-heavy. I stretched against the wrist restraints, but there was no give. A train whistle cut through the air. People spoke in low voices just outside the tent. The red and blue police lights threw around odd colored shadows.

"Thank you, Mary. My name is Dr. Ferrad. You remember me, don't you? I'm so sorry this has happened to you, but we don't have much time. You must tell us where your friends are, how many people did you injure, everywhere you've been and—"

"Help," I said, my voice cracking. The *h* sound groaned under the weight of my tongue. The rest of the word barely made it out around the swelling in my throat.

"We can help you." She stood up, unwrinkling the folds so that the suit ballooned out as if air was being blown inside. Maybe it was. She had one of those tanks strapped to her back.

But something in her words—I didn't believe it. They hadn't helped the creep who'd sprayed blood in my eye or the axe murderer who'd bitten me. Or rather, they had helped him, but I didn't want that kind of help. Not for my friends.

I shook my head, flinging a strand of saliva onto the ground. Embarrassment filled me as my body betrayed me. I was going to die here. If moon suit didn't kill me first.

The guard, for that's what I decided he must be, stepped forward, a type of stick appearing in his hand. Except it wasn't a normal stick because it crackled with the sound of electricity.

"No, Sergeant Bennings," she said. "It will only trigger an amygdala response."

"Your way is not working either," he said, his voice muffled by the filter as if he talked through a pillow.

He hovered closer to me, stick outstretched. "It worked before with the other one."

"It did not work before. You sent him into a rage that generated enough adrenaline in his body that he broke out of his restraints!"

"He told us what we needed. There is too much at stake here, Dr. Ferrad, to pretend this is some science experiment. I have been authorized—"

She stepped in front of the stick, inches away from me now, from my fingers. Her suit billowed at her movement and then resettled.

Sweat broke out on my face. My palms became slippery. I wriggled my fingers and brushed the plastic fabric. If she stepped close, I could grab it and tear into it and get to what was inside of it and teach her a lesson for locking me up like this.

"Get out of the way," he said.

"I will not."

There was a crackle and buzz and then a sharp gasp. She crumpled and fell onto me, enveloping me in a cloud of white. Parts of the suit deflated and parts of her hit me, and parts of me hit her on her way to the ground. She slithered into a heap, as if someone had thrown water on the Wicked Witch of the West.

He stepped around her and came at me with the stick. I trembled in my chair from excitement. He held it outstretched from his body and pointed it straight at my nose. The electricity raised the hairs on my face and sent an energy thrumming through me. It didn't matter that I hadn't eaten all day. Something else was powering me now and all he needed was to step a little closer and I would catch his suit in my fingers too.

Something crackled. He looked away, down onto the heap of cloth that had become a person sitting up, legs straight out, gloved hand holding a radio to the helmet face.

Another moon suit opened the flaps and ordered the stick-man out. The stick-man left as if lit on fire.

"That is not the way to get what we need," new moon suit said. "Please proceed. I will remain as your second for now."

"Thank you." She rose up from the ground and brushed the dirt off her formerly-pristine suit.

"Hold," he said, command filling his voice. "There is damage." He said this in a quieter voice, but it sounded like judgment raining down.

She froze, arms outstretched, body like a marshmallow. "Oh my god, where?"

"In the back. Near your hip. A three-inch-wide slit. I can see the garment underneath—it's also damaged…There is blood."

A long silence and I wondered if I had ripped it. I didn't think I'd touched her suit. I only imagined it. She had stayed out of my reach. It must have been when she fell. It must have been.

"It's nothing," she said. "I have not been near the subject. Nowhere close."

"You would risk…?"

"I…" She turned away, back again, in a circle, looking for a way out and finding none.

"You will get the best care. We will not rest until we have solved this." He held out his hand for the radio still in hers.

She drew her arm away.

"You have witnessed the research. You know there is not much time," he said.

Even though a suit covered her body, something about her posture changed. She slumped down in defeat. She handed him the radio. "I understand."

He walked to the far end of the tent and spoke quickly.

She began undoing the various layers, removing the gloves, unlatching the helmet, lifting it off her head to reveal thick chestnut curls cut close to her scalp. Her blue eyes under the orange-rimmed glasses looked haunted, her lips were set in a grim line, stress wrinkles surrounded her mouth. She looked like she was in her late thirties. She looked competent and authoritative and like a lost little girl all at once.

"You must tell us," she said again, no helmet distorting her face or voice anymore. She reached for what I thought had been a tray of medical tools, but now saw held a container of hypodermic needles. She tore a needle from its sterile packaging, inserted it into a vial, and drew out the liquid.

"I am going to tell you the truth and it's not going to be pretty," she said. "We can't save you. Too much time has passed. But there is a cure…There's a way for us to help your friends, or anyone you've infected—"

"I am…no…snitch—"

"We have to give them the injection within two hours or the initial infection gets too much of a head start. That's our window. You have to let us fix this before it spreads any further. You have to tell us where your friends are." She injected herself in the arm and winced as she pushed down on the plunger. She withdrew the needle, tossed it into a metal receptacle, and rubbed the injection. Then she just waited.

My brain felt like it was full of blood-soaked cotton. She was asking me to lock my friends up. She was asking me to destroy their dreams, their freedom, to be the one who put them back into the system we'd all run from.

Then I realized I had already done worse to them than that, by my own hands, my own mouth. I'd infected them with this virus. I had waited too long to run.

Now my friends had to pay with everything that still mattered to us.

WHEN IT'S TIME TO GO

Posted August 10th at 8:49PM on Do More Than Survive: How to THRIVE as a Runaway

Become a really good observer. Notice when people start staring at you (time to go). Notice when a cop gives you a second look (time to go). Notice when the other runaways and homeless and prostitutes you are used to seeing are no longer around (time to go).

Notice when the friends you make on the street become worse than the family you left behind (time to go).

Notice when you are the friend on the street worse than the family they left behind (time for you to go).

Remember that no matter how big or small your dreams are for your life and your future and for the people around you that you care about—the street will eat them all and there won't even be crumbs left behind for your dog to lick.

4

"SHED."

"You last saw them at a shed?"

"Here."

"At a shed here at the train station?"

I nodded.

"How long ago?"

I shook my head even though it made the tent spin.

"You don't know. Okay, that makes sense. The virus distorts perception of time. How many have you infected?"

I tried to think back, only my friends, all my friends, all our dreams for the future. "Six. All of them." A tear slipped down my cheek, but I couldn't wipe it away with my hands strapped down. It stayed there for all the world to see, to know, to despise.

She counted out the vials and separated them from the box.

The other suit returned and she filled him in. He rested a glove on her bare shoulder for a moment.

"You will need to decontaminate that now," she said.

He returned to the far side of the tent and spoke again into the radio. The responding voice, crackling with static, was recognizable. Officer Hanley.

A keening noise started, and then I realized it came from me, from my throat. I thrashed in the chair, raising my hips and stomach, lurching like a caterpillar rising from a leaf, but the straps kept me in place even as the moon suit jumped back into the folds of the tent.

Someone outside yelled, and then there were footsteps. I settled back into the chair, my tantrum doing nothing. Moon suit shouted everything was fine, it was fine, stay away, and then the steps went away.

"I promise you this will save your friends. They will be getting the same treatment as me," she said. But something else hitched in her voice and told me that whatever this treatment did, it wasn't much better than death.

She wavered on her feet, as if swaying to slow music. She pressed her hand to the back of her forehead and closed her eyes. "It works so quickly, so damn quickly."

She opened her eyes and looked at me, as if trying to read whether there was anything human left inside of me. I thought there was, but not much, not enough.

She grabbed a needle, emptied a vial into it, plunged the liquid into my IV, then did this a second and a third time.

"What are you doing?" he said. "We are losing control over this thing. We can't waste our resources."

"It probably won't work," she said, not really answering him, I think, but more answering the question in my eyes. "It hasn't yet worked this long after, but I had to try..." The needle and vials fell out of her hands and she swayed again, this time with her eyes closed, as if she had fallen asleep standing up. Moon suit caught her just as she went down, softening her fall to the ground. He laid her out carefully and then jumped back and checked over his suit as if it were covered with red fire ants.

When he could not find a tear or hole, his hands came to rest at his sides. He heaved deep breaths, almost sobbing, but there was no sound except for the rustling of his clothes and the low, soft hiss of his air tank.

I closed my eyes and swam in a sea of red. Metal dinged against metal, steps sounded, a plastic tent flap rustled.

I opened my eyes and saw he was gone and had taken the tray of vials with him.

▪

She sat up and crawled a few feet away, her hands and knees dragging in the dirt like she had weights tied to them.

"What's happening?" she asked.

My throat closed up again. My damn throat. It itched but the straps kept me from relieving it and this set a fire in my stomach and I pulled hard on the straps.

The left strap loosened an inch.

She looked around, dazed, as if not seeing who spoke and then locked eyes on me before drifting away to look at something on the tent wall. I craned my neck and saw nothing.

There was nothing to see, nothing that deserved the attention she gave it, as if she were watching someone who was about to die.

But she wasn't looking at me.

"It wasn't supposed to turn out like this," she said. Talking to the tent wall. "I know," she said, as if in response to someone. "I understand, we all understand. It was an unexpected mutation. Clearly, no one thought—"

She looked to the side, as if ashamed. "It's the only chance you've got, but it will make it impossible not to remember. You'll remember everything and sometimes all at once and —"

She went silent, as if listening. Then, "That's a possibility. But the psychologist will be here. There's no guarantee, but you're strong. You're not going to go crazy."

I worked at the left strap and it relaxed a little more. A low buzzing started in the tent as if someone had flipped on a generator from far way. I looked around, trying to place the direction. A roar of blood rushed into my ears and should have blocked the buzzing, but it didn't. The noise grew louder.

I realized the buzzing came from inside me. Inside my mind.

"We have a plan," she said, barely cutting through the noise in my head. "Camp Mendocino. We'll be taking you there and it will be okay. We'll find a real cure." Tears streamed down her face. She kept her eyes open, unblinking, and didn't wipe away the wetness. She pantomimed giving someone a shot in the arm. She caressed the air and moved her fingers as if pushing aside a stray tendril of hair. "Drink some water while you still can." She grabbed an imaginary cup and gently, like handling a baby, brought it to someone's mouth and tipped the cup in her hand. "I'll be here the whole time. I won't leave. I promise."

She set the cup down on the dirt and the tears kept flowing and she crossed her arms around her knees and rocked back and forth.

As if someone had flipped a switch, she slumped over. Her breath stayed heavy and uneven. Her forehead glistened with sweat and flushed with fever.

She'd gone crazy, but I felt crazier, because the buzzing kept rising, became insistent and I needed to do something, anything to make it stop.

▪

A hazy pink film lay over my vision like a vintage photo filter, but somehow it made everything clear. No wavy lines, though the fire in my stomach and my head remained. The buzzing was there too, but more pleasant now, tickling me. A woman lay on the dirt. A slight breeze moved the tent flaps. Voices rumbled outside.

My eyes felt lazy, as if waiting to lock on to something, as if something important was about to happen. Saliva filled my mouth and part of me understood that it dripped down my chin and dribbled onto the dirt. Most of me did not notice.

I felt distant from my body, as if down a long tunnel from the me I used to be. The girl who laughed and made her friends laugh, the girl who had been hurt and then loved anyway. The girl who always put herself between her friends and danger. The girl who dreamed about living in a Garden of Eden with her friends. The girl who will forever be upset with herself for not finishing high school, for not going to even one school dance. But this desire, this regret danced away into a hot fog and I couldn't remember why I felt it.

Figures blocked the tunnel path. Shapes, bodies, six of them, and another, a seventh body in a white suit. The others were dark, even though the light shined.

The others were familiar.

I knew them from somewhere. Dark boxes, rumbling train wheels, laughing at an oogle—memories on the tip of my tongue and then I swallowed and they disappeared and the pain in my throat returned. Confusion buzzed up like a bee. I shrank away from it, flinching, swatting at it. But my hands didn't move. The buzzing increased and filled my head as if a swarm of bees kept running into each other, running into the sides of my skull, darting backward and forward again.

"She told us where you were," white suit said.

"She wouldn't have done that," one of the dark bodies said.

"Look at her. She doesn't want you to turn into this."

Silence, except for the buzzing, that damn buzzing. Gabbi would laugh when I told her this new craziness that had started in my head. First talking to myself, now a bunch of insects haunting me. Was Gabbi here? I peered at each person. Sullen faces, bloody bites, kids my age, but I couldn't place them. Familiar, but—

The woman on the ground twitched. A shudder went through her body. The group jumped back as if coming unexpectedly upon the edge of the cliff.

"I've allowed you to see her, to see what could happen, but there's not much time."

The tallest one, the one with light eyes and a steady look that never wavered from my face—he stepped forward. The edges of his body smeared as if he were in a painting. "Give me the shot."

"There will be recovery time. We will take care of you—"

"I understand. Give me the shot."

White suit pulled out a needle and vial. It bothered me that I knew the voices but not the names of those faces. Gabbi would be angry with me for forgetting like this.

The suit injected the group one by one. They talked low among themselves so I could not hear the words over the buzzing and this made me want to shout at them to speak up or else I was going to punch somebody.

One of the bodies dropped like a feather to the ground. The others helped each other to sit.

As if by magic, a strap gave way and my wrist was free and the white suit hadn't seen because he was too busy checking wrists and necks and spreading out legs as people fell over from their cross-legged positions.

I become free of the other strap, and then the ankle straps gave way like they never existed. I fell out of the chair and on the ground next to the one who was still cross-legged. There were shouts, movement, shadows against the tent fabric. Something pulled at me and I turned and my mouth opened and I chomped down on something fleshy, and a part of me, that distant part, far away down the dark tunnel, gagged, but most of me didn't.

I turned back to the dark face, the face going dark in front of me, the face that was both familiar and strange and the face that made me both sorry and angry because I wanted to know who it was, I wanted to remember who, I wanted to remember this feeling that was nothing more than an empty bowl because it used to be important, it used to mean everything to me but I can't remember. I can't, I can't, I can't.

Gabbi.

Her eyes were wide, her brown irises so clear I could see the texture. Her pupils were huge and black and the whites of her eyes showed that she was more scared than I have ever seen her except for that night it stormed and we first met her, holed up in a house that might as well have been haunted, with a mother and father worse than being haunted.

"Mary?"

I heard my name and her voice saying my name and this was familiar enough and I remembered how much I cared about her, how many times I told her to lighten up, how the world was full of bad things but also a lot of good things too. I remembered all the times I made her laugh and all the other times I tried to make her laugh and then those memories fell away. As soon as I thought them someone plucked the threads from my brain and threw them aside and I could not get them back no matter how much I wished. The desire to wish them back faded and I realized the world was a bad place, the world was full of darkness and people hurting people and turning on people and becoming animals and turning on each other like animals.

And then like a lightning strike—I did not have much time left because soon it would all be gone, all the memories, all the feelings.

"Kill me," I said. I think I said it. I hope it came out, but I could not hear it. Only I knew I must have said it because she, this girl I was supposed to know, this girl whose name started with a G, I think, her eyes went impossibly wide and she shook her head and said, "No. No, Mary."

Suits rushed into the tent but milled around, almost afraid, almost tripping over themselves not to be the first one to me.

"Do it," I snarled.

She shrank. This little girl shrank from me as if I had hit her.

I stumbled backwards and cupped my mouth and felt the saliva, cold and wet on my chin. Never. I would never. I would never.

I took another step and another. Someone yelled and grabbed my shoulders.

His face. His brown eyes. This was Ano and I held that name in my mind with all my strength. I would not lose this name because this name had always spoken kind words to me. He had stood between Jimmy and me when I had turned dangerous. I wish I could have been as courageous.

I wish I could remember where I had seen those eyes before. I was supposed to tell those eyes something. It had been important.

The buzzing returned and I swore there were insects in the tent. They were landing on my head, my forehead, my arms, crawling inside my ears and nose and mouth to get to the other insects already inside my empty cave of a brain.

And then my brain cleared and I saw all of their faces and knew all of their names and knew I was still a danger to them. This anger filled me and made me want to destroy things. I would destroy them.

Run away. This distant voice said from down a far, far tunnel. It was a trustworthy voice. It was my own voice.

Run away, my voice said again.

I clawed through the tent fabric and it was dark on the other side except for the street lights that threw orange rays onto the pavement—and the trains.

I ran away from the tent. I ran for the trains while I could still remember their names.

I ran away.

A whistle pierced the sky. People shouted. The train chugged forward.

The train picked up speed and ate up the yards between it and me and the horn blew again and the white headlight consumed the night sky and the ground. I would jump while I could still remember to jump. I would put the train between me and my friends.

I was always the one to keep them safe and this would keep them safe, from me.

I jumped.

REMEMBER THE RED PLACE

Posted September 29th at 6:30PM on Do More Than Survive: How to THRIVE as a Runaway

We don't know if you're really gone or not. But if you're not, maybe you'll read this and know we are all still alive because of you. Mary, you gave us a real chance. We got the cure and it's, well it's not awesome, but it's better than what you went through. We want you to know they had us inside for weeks, but they took care of us, and when things got crazy Spencer got us out. Ano helped. He says to text that he misses you.

I miss you too—this is Gabbi.

To anyone else reading this. They're trying to deny everything and pretend that it's under control. They don't have it under control. Maybe they did for awhile, but that isn't the truth any longer.

Mary—if somehow you are still alive and aren't a crazy V, meet us at the place. You know the one. The red place in the field. We'll look different but it'll still be us.

To the rest of you. Don't bother leaving a comment asking where it is. We won't tell you.

FIND OUT WHERE THE RED PLACE IS... IN BOOK 1.

GERMINATION (BOOK 0)
CONTAMINATION (BOOK 1)
INFESTATION (BOOK 2)
ERADICATION (BOOK 3)

Get the complete ZOMBIES ARE HUMAN series in ebook, paperback, and audio

Ordering information at

books.jamiethornton.com/zombies

ABOUT THE AUTHOR

Jamie Thornton is a *New York Times* and *USA Today* bestselling author of post-apocalyptic science fiction. She lives in Northern California with her husband, two dogs, a garden, lots of chickens, a viola, and a bicycle. Her stories take place halfway around the world, in an apocalyptic future, in a parallel universe—and always take the reader on a dark adventure.

Join the Adventure through her email list to receive freebies, discounts, and information on more of her dark adventures.

Sign up at

JAMIETHORNTON.COM

ZOMBIES ARE HUMAN

Special EBOOK and AUDIO box sets

Once upon a time a plague ended the world. Four tough, young women. An apocalypse (or two). Powerful enemies, twisted memories, a government willing to do anything for control.

The completes series available now in ebook, paperback, and audio

Dessa has plans.

She plans to stay out of trouble in the group home where she lives. She plans to work crazy hours at the grocery story to save for her own place. She plans to get her little brother back, soon, from his foster parents.

But when a zombie apocalypse arrives, it wrecks all of Dessa's plans. With the city falling into chaos, Dessa must use her street smarts to survive. Her only weapon against the zombies is a pillowcase of tuna cans. Her only allies are the other group home teens she doesn't dare trust.

And there's only one plan left in the entire universe that matters.

Find and save her brother before it's too late.

AFTER THE WORLD ENDS is a new series in the same best-selling universe as ZOMBIES ARE HUMAN.

Available Now in ebook, paperback, and audio

Made in the USA
Las Vegas, NV
04 October 2023

78539837R00059